Hacker!

a novel

by

ALEX KROPP

H·I·P Books

Library and Archives Canada Cataloguing in Publication

Kropp, Alex, 1979–
Hacker! / Alex Kropp.

(New Series Canada)
ISBN 1-897039-09-3

I. Title. II. Series.

PS8621.R66H33 2005   jC813'.6   C2005-900836-9

General editor: Paul Kropp
Text design: Laura Brady
Illustrations drawn by: Catherine Doherty
Cover design: Robert Corrigan

    2 3 4 5 6 7   07 06 05 04 03 02

Printed and bound in Canada

High Interest Publishing is an imprint of the Chestnut Publishing Group

Computer crime hits a high school, and the prime suspect is a teacher. Hacker and Cole have to find who's behind the mess before the football team breaks them in two.

CHAPTER 1

A Nasty Surprise

"What?" I screamed at the computer. "What the...?"

My partner in the computer lab looked over at me. "Cole, that really sucks," he said, looking at my screen.

Our computer teacher, Mrs. Layton, had just put our marks online. Now, I wasn't expecting a great mark. I'm no computer geek. I'm not a guy who cracks code in his spare time. There was no way I'd be up with my friend Hacker at the top of the class. Still, nothing could have gotten me ready for the mark that I saw. There it was on the screen: a 38.

I flunked!

"You should have a higher mark than that," Hacker went on.

I just sat there, shaking my head. I could already picture Dad when he found out. He'd give me this awful grin he used when I screwed up. The one that screamed out, "I told you so." This would no doubt be followed by yet another lecture about the smart kid next door. And another lecture about me, the football meathead.

"I'm toast," I grumbled.

Hacker wasn't listening to me. He seemed more interested in my mark than in his own. Hacker is like that — kind of curious. His real name is Hakaru. It means something like "man who thinks things through" in Japanese. He's only half-Japanese, and the other half is Italian. But Hacker does think about things step by step.

I was about to close the browser when Hacker stopped me.

"Hold on a second," he said. "Make a printout of this page so we can check the marks." Hacker hit the print command and soon grabbed the printout from the laser printer.

I just groaned. "Layton probably did all this with a spreadsheet. Computers don't make mistakes."

"Maybe not," Hacker replied, "but people do. Computers only do what people tell them to. They're just machines, Cole. Not even as smart as you — though that wouldn't be hard."

I was about to lace into him for the insult when Mrs. Layton came into the lab. "All right, everyone, take your seats. We are going over the midterm grades today." Mrs. Layton was a teacher who had no sense of humour. It was like she was always in a bad mood.

Mrs. Layton gave us the same speech we heard in all our classes. It was all that junk about how much each assignment was worth towards the final grade. Most of us tuned her out. She kept on saying things like, "Even if you have a bad mark now, you still have half the term to make it up." I felt as if she was looking straight at me every time she said it.

"There are a couple of students in here who deserve special notice," Mrs. Layton went on. "I'm sure no one is surprised to hear that Hakaru was near perfect with a 97," she looked over at my buddy. "But there were a few surprises as well."

Nicole Holden, the class big mouth, seemed ready to burst. She was looking at Spike Gruber's screen, amazed. Then she had to spit it out. "Spike got a 92!" she squeaked.

The class was shocked enough to wake up. A buzz of voices filled the room. Spike Gruber had aced the course! How could that happen? Spike was about as smart as a brick. No, he was worse — about as smart as a concrete block.

But Spike just flashed a smile like he had scored a winning touchdown just as the clock ran out.

"All right, that's enough," Mrs. Layton said, making a shushing motion with her hands. "Spike did do well. That should show you all how a little hard work will pay off. You just have to get down to it."

"Spike never worked hard in his entire life," I whispered to Hacker. "Something about this stinks."

Hacker just nodded. He was still looking over my marks.

Both of us had problems with Spike. It started way back in Grade 6 when Hacker first moved in. Spike was a real bully back then and did his best to beat the snot out of my buddy. He never quite got the chance to finish the job, but Hacker took the hint. By Grade 7, my friend was lifting weights and taking some martial arts classes. Now he had bigger muscles than most of my buddies on the football team. Not bad for someone who used to be a scrawny little Asian kid.

I sat through the rest of the lecture feeling totally out of it. If Spike can land a 92 and Hacker can get a 97, then what is wrong with me?

When Mrs. Layton finally finished, she said we could use the rest of our class time to work on our projects. That gave Hacker a chance to talk to me about my term mark.

He turned to me with a funny look on his face. "Cole, what did you get on that big project I helped you with? The one that's worth 10 percent of our grade."

"I can't remember," I admitted. "It was a good enough mark. Definitely a B . . . maybe a low 70?"

"Well, your printout here says you only got a 44. Do you still have the copy you got back? We can check the mark against the grade on the project itself."

I looked a little sheepish. "You know me. I have no idea where it is."

Hacker sighed. "Cole, you'd lose your head if it wasn't attached to your neck with a little too much muscle."

"I'll probably lose my head when my parents see this mark," I moaned.

I sure felt like my head was on the chopping block. My father was the man with the axe. I had worked so hard on these computer projects that my brain felt fried. And for what? A lousy 38. I felt a little sick to my stomach when I thought of all the work going down the tubes. All that wasted time.

"We'll ask Layton to check her mark book," offered Hacker. He was trying to cheer me up.

"Forget it," I told him. "Maybe some miracle will give me a passing grade by the end of the term.

Good thing the football season is over or I'd be pulled off the team. After my parents see this, they'll ground me, like, forever. At least I'll have plenty of time to study."

"You really shouldn't accept a failing grade without checking it out, you know," Hacker went on. Good advice, I guess, but I wasn't listening.

I had just opened my mouth to answer him when that jerk Spike walked over to us. "So," he said with this awful smile on his face, "how did you do, Cole?"

"Just great," I lied. "Just shows what hard work can do." There was no way I'd admit my mark to someone like Spike.

"Yeah, right," he said with a laugh. "The way you're going, you'll be a rocket scientist in no time."

Hacker rolled his eyes and looked up at Spike. "Hey, Spike, why don't you do us a favor and go play in traffic. There's some big truck out there that's just looking for a target."

Spike looked very angry, but he wasn't stupid enough to mess with Hacker. He went back to his own computer.

At least my day can't get any worse, I thought. I'm already at the bottom of the barrel.

But I was wrong. The barrel was deeper than I thought. I wouldn't even see the bottom until the end of class. That's when a voice came over the PA system.

Cole Walsh please report to the office. Cole Walsh to the office. . . .

CHAPTER 2

Missing Three Grand

"How's it going, Ms. Hawthorne?" I asked the principal as I came into the office. Since I've become captain of the football team, I've gotten to know the principal so well I can almost call her by her first name. Well, almost.

Ms. Hawthorne looked hard at me. "I wish it were going better, Cole. We need to have a chat. A serious one."

That was my first clue that something was

wrong. Then I noticed the second clue. Ms. Hawthorne's office has great big glass windows that look out into the main office. When nothing is going on, the curtains stay open. It's only when a kid gets called in for something bad that the curtains are closed. Today, those curtains were shut tight.

"Cole, I think you had better sit down," said Ms. Hawthorne.

"I can tell something is wrong, Ms. H," I began. "What's the matter?"

This was way different from the last time I was sitting in the office. The last time was the day after our team fundraiser. The football team put on this great dance with live music and laser lights. We managed to rake in over three thousand bucks. Since we were using the money for new uniforms, the school board and the Rotary Club agreed to match the money we made. That gave us just over nine grand for new stuff.

Not to blow my own horn, but I was a hero for pulling the whole thing off. Even my dad had to admit that I'd done a great job.

But now Ms. Hawthorne was looking at me like I was something she scraped off the bottom of her shoe.

"Tell me," she said leaning forward on the desk. "How much money did you make with the dance last week?"

I felt a bit like a prisoner being grilled. "Um . . . just over three thousand dollars last time I looked," I replied. "Hacker — I mean, Hakura — he helped me check the numbers."

She smiled a very thin smile and tapped her chin

with a finger. "You're sure there was no mistake?"

"Totally. I don't think Hacker has made a mistake in years," I said with a big grin on my face.

Ms. Hawthorne didn't look pleased. "Cole, you know I believed those numbers you gave me. I even have the cheques right here from the school board and the Rotary Club."

"So what's the problem?" I asked her.

"I just got the final statement back from Mrs. Layton. Take a look at the figures for yourself. This covers all the money going in and out of the student council account this month." She passed me a piece of paper.

I quickly scanned the printout until I found the date for the day after the dance. I traced my finger from the date column to the deposits.

"Impossible!" I shouted. "It says $258.76. It's three thousand dollars short!"

"Now you understand why I called you in here. You say that the dance made $3258.76, but the computer record says $258.76."

I shook my head. "That's just not possible. There were about 500 people there, give or take. It was five bucks a ticket to get in. The band was made up of students, so they played for free. We ran a coat check at a buck a pop. Plus we sold drinks and snacks. The only things we even had to pay for were the refreshments and the police guard. I mean, it was the best dance this school has ever had."

"I know all of that, Cole. When you said that we had made over three thousand I hadn't doubted you at all. It's just that now with these numbers . . . well, who are people going to believe? Computers don't make mistakes."

It seemed to me I had even said that myself.

Ms. Hawthorne went on, "I know we should have made more money on this dance. It's obvious that something went wrong somewhere. I just have to know what happened to the money, and fast. If this isn't cleared up within a week I'm going to have to return this money to the board and the Rotary Club. So I need some answers, Cole."

"But, Ms. Hawthorne ..." I moaned. I didn't even know what to say at this point. "Nothing could have gone wrong. Look, I'll go over all the numbers with Hacker again. Maybe someone just hit the minus key instead of the plus."

"Cole, for your sake I hope that's true. I'll give you until the start of next week. If the money doesn't turn up by then, my hands will be tied. I'll have to return all the money. Not only that, but I'll have to explain what happened to your team, and I don't think they'll be happy with the news."

I gulped. My team wouldn't just be unhappy, they'd break me in two.

"I'll find the problem, Ms. Hawthorne," I said. "You can trust me, really you can."

"I hope so, Cole," she replied with a sigh. "I truly hope so."

I stumbled out of the office in a daze. Three thousand bucks had just disappeared, and all because of some lousy computer mistake. That stunk! But then I thought about what the guys on the team would do to me when they found out. No new uniforms. No money from the dance. And it was all my fault.

I wondered if any doctor in the world would be able to fix that many broken bones. I began to

think about my new life as a jelly-like blob.

Just then I ran into something that felt like a brick wall. When I looked over, it was just Hacker. I had walked straight into him without even noticing.

"Cole, are you all right?" he asked me. "You look so out of it."

"Hacker, I'm so dead," I said. "You remember the dance last week?"

"Yeah, probably the best thing you ever did."

I leaned in to whisper so the other students

wouldn't hear. "We are exactly three thousand dollars short of what should have gone into the bank."

"You're kidding," he said.

I shook my head so he knew I was serious.

Hacker just got this look on his face. I had never seen a look like that before. For maybe the first time in his life, I think Hacker felt stupid.

CHAPTER 3

Better for My Health

The bell for the next class rang and the hall filled with kids. It was clear that Hacker and I couldn't talk about the problem just then. The fewer people who heard about it, the better. At least, the better for my health.

"Why don't you meet me in the weight room after last class," Hacker said.

"The weight room? Hacker, we're in real trouble here. This is not the time to go pumping iron."

"That's why we're going to lift some weights," he answered. "It helps calm you down. Besides, no one ever goes there after school except me. It'll be the perfect place to figure this out."

I handed him the computer printout that Ms. Hawthorne gave me earlier. Maybe he could find something there that I couldn't see. Then I spent the rest of the day worrying. I know I didn't learn anything at all after my meeting with the principal. All I could see was me in the Kingston jail. I could see me turned into ground beef by the football team. I could see me lying in a coffin and no one at the funeral.

I tried to find a small ray of hope somewhere, anywhere, but it just wouldn't come to me. I could already see my father's face. I could picture the look he'd give me when he found out the news.

When the school day was over, I made my way to the school's weight room. Of course, rumours had already leaked to the football team. I had to try and avoid them as best I could. I didn't want to answer any questions that my buddies might want to ask. I had a hunch their questions wouldn't be very friendly.

When I got to the gym, Hacker was benching some free-weights. "What took you so long?" he asked.

"I was trying to avoid my team," I explained. "I think word has already gotten out. I ran into Maniac on the way here and he wanted to have a chat."

Maniac was the name we gave to Manny Jones. He had earned his nickname as a tackle on our team. He could, and probably would, crush me with one arm if the money didn't turn up.

"What did he want?" Hacker asked. He was pushing up more than 50 kilograms on the bench, and it didn't even look as if he was trying hard.

"I'm sure you can guess. If the new uniforms don't come in next month, he says I'd better move to the Yukon. For my health."

"Don't buy . . ." Hacker let out his breath as he lifted the weight once more, ". . . your plane ticket yet." He lowered the weight onto the stand. "I may just have an answer."

I felt some hope for the first time since the morning. "If you've got one, I'll owe you big time."

"You already owe me big time. Besides, I haven't got the money . . . nor am I sure which person does."

"So?" I asked, waiting for the explanation.

"Get on the bench, Cole. See if you can press 30 kilograms." He had changed both plates on the barbell for me.

I groaned. "My life is at stake and you want me to lift weights?" I swear, Hacker is really strange sometimes.

"Come on, Cole. Lifting weights is good for you," he explained. "It will help to relieve your stress. I doubt you've ever been as stressed out as you are today. Besides, you'll need the muscle if Maniac and the rest of your team are going to come after you."

"I thought you said you had an answer for me?" I grunted as I lifted the bar off of the stand.

"I have an answer to one question, but not an answer to the big question," he said. "I looked over that printout you gave me. The simple truth is that the student council bank account is out three grand. It's pretty clear that the figures we turned in were changed *after* they were put in the computer."

"So?" I asked. I breathed in deeply as I let the weight back down to my chest. Football or not, I didn't need to be a huge guy to play quarterback. I wasn't used to this weightlifting business.

"So, the principal plainly thinks that you or I took that money for ourselves," was his reply.

"But we didn't." I strained under the weights some more.

"Of course not," Hacker replied. "Even if we did, it would hardly be worth stealing three thousand bucks if you'd have to spend it on plane tickets to the Yukon."

"So what good is this?" I asked. I gave up on the weights and put the bar back on the stand. "All you've shown me is that we're the most likely suspects. I don't need your brain to figure that one out."

"When you have a problem, it's important to lay out all of the information that you have," he said. His namedoesn't mean "man who thinks hrough" for nothing. "Number One: We didn't take the money. Number Two: Whoever took it knows how to break into the school's computer system."

"You forgot number three," I said, "If those are all the facts we have, I'm dead. There has to be something else that we're missing."

That sick feeling in my gut was coming back in full force. I don't think it had anything to do with lifting weights.

"Well, there is that 92 in computers that Spike got," Hacker went on. "There's something really strange about that. I'm not saying it's connected, but you never know."

I took a drink of water from the fountain next to the gym office. "You might be right, but unless Spike has three grand in his wallet it doesn't help us much."

"True enough," said Hacker, "But what about this? Not only does Mrs. Layton handle the school's computer system, but she also does the bank deposits for student council."

"And she doesn't like me," I added.

"Layton doesn't like anybody. You just made me think of one thing, though."

"What's that?"

"That whoever took the money doesn't like you

and wants to make it look like you stole it." Hacker looked thoughtful for a second. "But then again, maybe not."

I rolled my eyes. "Hacker, you're driving me insane. We haven't got a lot of time. By Tuesday there will be pieces of me all over the school grounds. My father will be going to each body part and yelling at it."

"That could be really ugly," Hacker agreed.

"And painful," I added. "What am I going to do?"

"Well, the first thing you're going to do is stop acting like it's only you involved. We're in this together, for better or worse. Since we both worked on those numbers, we're both marked for death."

"Real cheerful, Hacker," I said.

"And I'm not trying to be insulting," he went on, "but if you go down for the lost money then all the kids will think I was the brains behind the plan."

That was true.

"There has to be a clue we can find somewhere," I said. "If we were cops, what would we look for? All I can think of is fingerprints, like in those bad cop

shows. But you can't exactly dust a computer for fingerprints."

Hacker's eyes lit up.

"That's it, Cole! You may have just accidentally given me a great idea. We might be able to find out who did this after all."

"What? How?" I stuttered.

"With a fingerprint!"

CHAPTER 4

Fingerprints at the Library

I think Hacker must have popped a few screws loose when he found out the bad news. I mean, how was he going to find a fingerprint on a computer? It sort of makes sense in those old cop shows where there's a murder victim and the body is still warm. But this was a computer crime. There was no way to go around looking for fingerprints.

But when Hacker gets an idea in his head, he

just goes all out. Nothing stops him until he gets some sort of answer. And I didn't have a choice — I needed his help.

"Come on," I pleaded. "At least tell me where we're going." He was in such a hurry that I barely had time to finish changing.

"We're going to find fingerprints," was all that he said. I figured his brain had finally fried itself. It had just been working too hard for too long and now it was toast.

Hacker came to a stop in front of the library, all the way on the other side of the school. Since it wasn't that late, the library was still open. As always, Lindsay Kilgour was working at the desk. She looked quite cool with her spiky hair and pierced eyebrows. Once upon a time I tried to go out with her. That was not a tale with a happy ending, though. That ending got even worse when she started going out with Spike Gruber.

Hacker waved at Lindsay and went straight for a row of computers in the back corner. I nodded to her and followed Hacker. He sat right down at a computer that was hidden from view. He stared

down at the keyboard. For a second I thought he was searching it for fingerprints.

"What are you doing?" I asked.

"Hmm . . . I need a program for this," he muttered.

"Uh, what?"

"Need the passwords file first."

"Are you okay?"

"Just need to log in."

I finally figured out that he was talking to himself. I guess he was just putting his thoughts together on what he had to do. There wasn't much I could do to help with that. There wasn't much anyone could do to help Hacker when it came to computers. I gave myself the job of keeping watch to make sure no one could see him.

After a few minutes, he stopped typing. "All right," he whispered, this time talking to me. "Now we just have to wait for a few minutes while the program does its job."

"So now will you explain it to me?" I asked.

"Sure," he said. "It's like this — all of these computers are connected by a network. From here, using the network, we should be able to gain access to the student council files. If we can break into the files, then maybe we can see what happened to the money."

"But you can't just hack into that kind of stuff," I said.

"See, you did learn something in computer class. Mrs. Layton has all of her files protected by a password. What you don't learn in computer class is that all the passwords are kept in a file on the main server. The passwords are scrambled so that you can't read them."

"So if the passwords are all scrambled, how are you going to use them?" I asked.

"That's why I have this program running." He pointed to a pop-up window on screen with a status bar slowly filling up. "This will try all the passwords it can make up over the next couple of minutes. It's called a 'Brute Force' program."

"Brute Force?" I asked.

"It's like taking a combination lock and trying to open it by trying ever number until you hit the right ones."

"But a combination lock only has three numbers. Our passwords are all eight letters long. This is going to take forever," I whined.

"Not so," explained Hacker. "This computer can try millions of combinations of letters and numbers in just a minute or two. Look, it's almost finished."

The status bar filled up and the window closed. A new window popped up showing Mrs. Layton's log-in name and her password. I was very impressed.

"So, can you break into any system with this thing?" I asked.

"Yes and no," Hacker replied. "I told this thing to only check for letters and numbers. If you start putting things in your password like periods or dollar signs, it can take longer. For every new character it has to check, it doubles the amount of time it takes to find it. So it could take you years to solve a really complex password." He jotted down a few notes. "Lucky for us, Mrs. Layton has a fairly simple password. If she were smarter, cracking the code would have taken longer."

The password looked to me like a random bunch of letters and numbers. Hacker entered this into the log-in screen. In seconds, we had broken into Mrs. Layton's computer account.

"What are you looking for now?" I asked.

"Now I'm looking for that fingerprint. All the teachers have much higher access levels to files than the students. I have more than enough power now to look at anything I want."

All I could do was scratch my head. He looked

like he was off in his own little world. I glanced up to see Lindsay walking towards us. As look-out, I had to distract her so Hacker could finish up.

I smiled my best smile as I headed her off. "Say, Lindsay, could you help me find a book? I'm looking for that new one by ..."

"Cole, who are you trying to kid? We all know that football players don't read," she said with a laugh. Lindsay sounded an awful lot like my father right then.

"As a matter of fact," I told her, "I've read quite a few books this year."

"Yeah, comic books don't count," she said. "What is Hacker up to over there?"

"Um . . . uh . . . I think he's trying out a new program he wrote."

"I'm supposed to keep an eye on the machines," Lindsay told me. "The librarian thinks that someone is using them to mess up her files."

"Some people have no respect," I said.

"No kidding. The other day I caught one of the janitors on the computer. I figured he was looking at porn. Then I found out he's been

taking courses in computers at night school."

"Maybe he's tired of being a janitor. Maybe he wants to get into computers and really clean up," I joked. I had to keep stalling Lindsay. Hacker was taking his time, whatever he was doing.

"I think computers are *so* dull," she said. "I mean, they're useful for typing out papers, but I just don't get guys like Hacker who are so into them. They're so . . ." she was looking for the right word.

"Geeky?" I offered.

"Yeah, even though Hacker is hardly your average geek."

"True enough," I replied. "Since you find computers so boring, I guess you didn't help Spike get that 92 in class."

"Spike doesn't need my help for anything," she said. "But I did hear that you're going to need help real soon. Like medical help."

"Oh? What did you hear?" I asked, playing dumb. Hacker was still staring at the computer screen.

"I heard something happened with the football uniform deal — something that stinks."

"Oh, and where did you hear that?" I started sweating a bit.

"Just a rumour, you know. A ton of people put a lot of work into that dance and they all expect to see something for it. I know Spike would go nuts if it fell through."

It seemed that I had stalled her for as long as I could. She pushed past me and stood behind Hacker, looking at the screen.

"What's this?" she asked him.

"Oh, just a new game I've been working on," Hacker said, cool as ice. "I call it *Missing Treasure*. You have to use the clues to find some lost money."

I looked at the screen and there it was. Hacker had made some 3D character go into a dungeon.

"I guess you really are a genius," sighed Lindsay. She shook her head and went back to her desk. With her out of the way I could finally find out what Hacker had found.

"Did you find it?" I whispered to him.

"Yeah," he said. "I believe we have found our fingerprint."

"And?" I was getting tired of all this.

"There was only one . . . and it belongs to Mrs. Layton."

CHAPTER 5

Waiting for the Other Hacker to Hack

I guess I should explain what Hacker was trying to say. As he told me, each time someone uses a file, it goes into the file history. What Hacker did was use Layton's access to check who the last person was to open the file. What he found was Layton's log-in name and the time and date of the last change.

Hacker also said he found something called a log file. It's a list that shows when anyone signs on or quits using the computers. He says the time and dates in the log file matched her fingerprint. As it turned out, the dance numbers were changed the day after we had sent them in.

"Then it was Mrs. Layton who did it," I said to Hacker. We were in his car, on the way to his house.

"Maybe, but I doubt it," he replied. "All we really have is a time and date that the data was changed," he said. "You remember how I gained access, right? I'm not the only guy who knows how to do that. So it may have been Layton, or it may have been someone else. So we have a suspect but we don't have any proof."

"Great," I muttered.

Hacker shrugged. "If it makes you feel better, I think we can start narrowing down the suspects."

"Will that stop Maniac and the rest of the team from beating me into a pulp?"

"Not until we find the money. We really need to find the hacker behind all this."

"Hacker?" I asked. "But you're Hacker."

"Not the nickname, but the real hacker — the person who broke into the system. Like so many things in life, there are different flavours of hacker. When I break into a system, I only do it to look around. I also cover up all my tracks. That's what a real hacker does."

I nodded in understanding.

"Now, the other kind of hacker are the jerk who only learns enough to trash a system. For him it's all about revenge rather than learning."

"I see," I said. "So how do we catch this trasher hacker?"

"Since we can't point cameras at every computer screen, I came up with another way. I installed a trojan into Mrs. Layton's account." Hacker spoke as if that would explain it.

"A what?"

Hacker glanced over at me. "A trojan is a special kind of program. This one is set so that any time someone logs in it will call me on my instant messenger. I can keep a running tab on the account from there. If someone and starts messing around with the file again, all we'll have to do is match the ID to the computer at school. If we're lucky, we can catch Mrs. Layton, or whoever,

red-handed. Then, my dear Mr. Watson, we have our man."

"Or woman," I said thinking of Mrs. Layton. "But what if the hacker doesn't go back on? She already has a couple thousand dollars. Maybe that's enough."

"No way," said Hacker. "An amateur like this is exactly the kind of person who returns to the scene of the crime. Since he was successful once, he'll feel safe to strike again."

"How do you know so much about this?" I said.

I mean, Hacker was smart, but he was no Sherlock Holmes.

"Let's just say I've spent enough time in seedy chat rooms to know what's what."

The next day I looked at Mrs. Layton with new eyes. I had never liked her very much before. Now I knew why. She had these small, beady eyes and there was something very strange about the way she acted. Like her mind was off someplace else. Maybe she was worried about getting caught.

When Mrs. Layton looked in my direction, I could feel the guilt coming off her in waves. Maybe she needed some cash for a laser eye fix-up or something. Teachers don't get paid much, do they? No matter, why put the blame on me? What did I ever do to her? Teachers do some nasty things to us kids sometimes, but this was a whole new low.

For his part, Hacker made sure his I.M. was always running. I'm not sure how he managed it, but he even set it up so that it would page his cell phone. Even so, it seemed unlikely that the hacker would risk getting caught on school time. After school the hacker could come in and do what she wanted. That old bat Layton could cover her tracks without being caught. Or so she would think.

It turned out that we were partly right. There were no pages sent to Hacker's phone during school. At night, we headed back to his place to watch the computer.

And we waited.

We had four days. They were counting down.

On Thursday we waited by the computer right through dinner time. At first we watched the screen, but that got old fast. Then we switched to some computer games. Then Hacker did some weightlifting and I ate half the food in his fridge. Of course, we talked.

"Maybe the hacker went out on a date," I said around eight o'clock.

"Hackers don't go on dates, Cole," he said.

"Then what do they do?" I asked.

"They make out with their DVD burners," he replied, and then laughed. "By the way, have you told your father about your mark in computers?"

"I thought I'd be better off waiting until the report comes in the mail," I replied. "He already thinks I'm dumb enough."

"Your dad expects a lot from you, eh?"

"Yeah. I think he wanted a genius son who could follow in his footsteps. Instead he ended up with me, a dumb jock."

"Come on, Cole. You're pretty smart in some things. And besides, half the kids and teachers at school like you. You shouldn't put yourself down all the time."

"Maybe you're right." I sat forward a bit. "You know what really bothers me? The way my dad compares me to that dork Erik Jones from next door. Eric is a real shining star, at least in my dad's eyes."

"You mean Maniac's little brother?" Hacker asked.

"Yeah. But you can't say anything to Maniac's face about it. It's pretty clear that Maniac got the brawn and Erik got the brains. I didn't get much of either."

"Or maybe you got a bit of both," he replied. Hacker looked over at the clock on the wall.

"So what do we do if the hacker does come back online?" I asked him, hoping to hear more of his plans.

"Then we go and catch the guy in the act," said Hacker.

"Yeah, but then what?"

"Well," Hacker thought to himself for a moment, "I suppose we confront him. I've got a camera built into my cell phone. We should have a picture of the guy doing whatever it is he's doing.

Then we tell the guy to come clean because we know his whole scheme … at least, we pretend to know it."

"Do we?"

"Probably not. Either way, whoever it is will still have a lot of explaining to do. The guy might confess right on the spot."

"Yeah, but what if the guy doesn't?"

"Then we … I don't really know," admitted Hacker. "Geez, Cole, you're being a real downer tonight."

He was right. "Well, hey," I said, trying to cheer up, "in the movies they always confess right on the spot right? 'You kids spoiled my perfect plan, so here it is in every detail.' Right?"

"Yeah, in the movies," Hacker sighed.

We were both quiet for a while. Each hour that passed was one less hour until I had to face what would happen on Monday.

Hacker looked as worried as I was. He didn't talk about it much, but he was in real trouble too. No one would think I had the brains to steal the money by myself. Hacker would be sure to get the blame. It might be the first time an honour student was kicked out of school and sent to jail. Just planting the trojan was against the law. The team might trash my body, but this thing might cost Hacker his whole future.

Just then, a window popped open on the computer and stopped all my thoughts.

"Is that the hacker?" I asked Hacker.

"Hold on," he said. "The guy only just logged in so I can't tell." Hacker looked at the status reports as they came in.

"There!" he shouted, jumping to his feet and knocking over his chair. "They just started accessing the student council files. Better still, they're accessing the bank files again."

"This is it! We've caught the guy," I yelled. "What computer is it?"

Hacker checked the computer ID number.

"It's Mrs. Layton's."

CHAPTER 6

Somebody Gets Caught

We got to school in five minutes flat. Hacker drove like a madman, weaving in and out of traffic and passing cars in the outside lane. If Hacker drove like this all the time, he'd probably beat any of the kids from school in a street race. Normally I'd have been screaming in fear. This time, he couldn't get there fast enough for my liking.

When we got there, the school was still open for night classes. There were a few people hanging around by the gym and pool, but the place was still pretty empty.

Hacker and I ran all the way from his car to the computer lab. We stopped just outside the door. Hacker looked through the little window on the door. He nodded and stepped aside for me. Guess who it was?

It was the terrible Mrs. Layton.

I looked at Hacker. The smile on my face said, "See? I told you so." I turned the doorknob and we stepped inside.

Mrs. Layton looked up from her computer. She was staring at us as if we were crazy.

I looked over at Hacker, hoping that he would say something but he seemed at a loss for words.

So Mrs. Layton spoke first. "Well, what brings you two here?" she asked.

I knew she had to be guilty. It was all in the way she acted, the way she tried to pretend nothing was wrong. But what were we supposed to do now?

"We . . . uh . . . we know what you're up to, Mrs. Layton," I said, trying to sound tough. Still, I got the feeling this wouldn't go down as easy as it does

in the movies. "Don't bother to try and cover your screen. We already know what you're doing," I said.

I didn't know if that was true or not. But hey, acting like we knew was Hacker's idea all along.

Hacker just stood there. His mouth was open but he wasn't saying anything, like he'd forgotten how to talk.

"You'll lose your job for this," I told her. "But If you come clean now, maybe you won't go to jail." I started to feel like the tough cop in those TV shows.

Mrs. Layton looked at me with a frown. "Cole, what on earth are you talking about?"

Hacker looked over at me, shaking his head. He was trying to tell me to shut up, but I couldn't figure that out. I just went ahead and crammed both my feet in my mouth.

"We know that you're taking money from the student council accounts. You might as well admit the whole thing to us," I told her.

Mrs. Layton was looking at me as if I had just escaped from some mental hospital.

"Hakaru, what is Cole going on about?" she asked.

Hacker was looking down at his feet, kind of embarrassed. "Um . . . we must have made a mistake, Mrs. Layton," he told her.

"We did?" I exploded. That sick feeling in my gut came back in full force.

"We did," Hacker said to me, his voice like the voice of doom. "As you know," he explained to Mrs. Layton, "someone has been changing the numbers in the school accounts."

"You're quite right," replied Mrs. Layton. "Your friend here is short three thousand dollars on that dance. I was just checking the numbers again to see if it was put in the wrong account. I haven't found any mistakes yet."

"You won't find a mistake," I told her. "Hacker . . . um . . . Hakaru checked the files three days ago. The money was stolen, and it was stolen by a hacker using your log-in."

She looked a little confused. "But you'd need my password for that. I'm the only one who knows it," she said.

"Well, Hacker made some sort of program . . . ," I began, and then I realized it was time to shut up.

My big mouth had got us in enough trouble already.

"You did what?" shouted Mrs. Layton, standing up beside the computer.

Hacker sighed. "I guess there's no sense in trying to hide it any more. I used a Brute Force program to crack your password, Mrs. Layton. I'm sorry, but we had no choice. And I found out that someone had broken into the files before me. That's the person who stole the football team's money."

"So you stole my password and broke into my files, eh?" said Mrs. Layton. She did not look pleased.

"We had to break in, Mrs. Layton," pleaded Hacker. "We knew it was wrong, but we were just trying to figure out who stole the money. I can even tell you just when the money was moved and how it was done. The only thing we don't know is who did it."

"So that's why you two came bursting in here like cops-and-robbers. You thought that I . . . " Boy, did she get angry when she figured it out. "You thought that I stole the money."

"I guess we were wrong," I said. I did my very best to shrink into my shoes.

"You couldn't be more wrong, young man. And you, Hakaru, broke into my personal account and the school's security files. You're smart enough to know how serious that is. How do I know that you two weren't just trying to cover up your own crime?"

"We didn't take any money," said Hacker.

"We're only trying to catch the guy who did," I

added. "There's someone in this school who's taken three grand and all the blame is on me."

"Maybe that's where the blame should be," Mrs. Layton said, still angry. "I want to see both of you in the principal's office first thing on Monday. You've got a lot of explaining to do. Not just to me and Ms. Hawthorne either. I'm bringing the police into this."

"But, Mrs. Layton — " I started.

"Enough," she cut me off. "You two had better use your weekend to plan what you're going to say on Monday. The principal and the police will want to hear a good story."

CHAPTER 7

Cole Gets a Brainwave

"Well, you were close, but no cigar," I said to Hacker. We walked down the hall, tails tucked between our legs. I knew we were worse off now than we were before, but I didn't want to say that out loud.

"I hate cigars anyway," Hacker groaned.

"I shouldn't have told Layton how we got into the files. That just added more trouble that we don't need."

"It's still no reason for her to bring in the cops," he said.

"Maybe it's just an empty threat," I offered.

Hacker just grunted in reply. "You know Mrs. Layton doesn't make idle threats. By Tuesday, the whole city will know about it."

"Yeah, we'll be on the front page of the *Waterloo Record*. TOP STUDENT KICKED OUT FOR COMPUTER CRIME."

"Make that, TOP STUDENT AND FOOTBALL CAPTAIN KICKED OUT," Hacker added. "I wonder if anyone will hire a computer genius with a jail record."

"You'd better learn how to push a broom," I said.

"Hey, let's look on the bright side," he replied, looking up. "There are worse things in life than jail."

"Like what?"

"Like . . . my parents could take away my computer," Hacker sighed.

"Think they would?" I asked.

"If we don't solve this mystery," Hacker said,

"they won't let me program the DVD. And you just worry about getting beaten up."

"I guess," I replied, not so sure about that one.

Only Hacker would worry more about losing his computer than getting his face mashed in. I was worried too. Not just about my health, but also about the police issue. Once the police came in I would never hear the end of it from my father. Never.

Hacker and I headed across the street to Tim Hortons. I bought Hacker a coffee and we sat down at a table to think, or worry, or both.

It was a pretty slow night at the coffee shop. There were only a few other people in the whole place. That included one guy pushing a mop near the entrance. I tried to picture Hacker doing the same job, but it just didn't fit.

We didn't say anything for a while. I'm not sure what Hacker was thinking about. As usual, I was thinking about the football team tearing me apart. It might be better if they beat me up so badly that I ended up in the hospital. Maybe it would even make my father feel sorry for me. Then again. . . .

"Let's get this worked out," Hacker said. His brain was working full force again, like a big V-8 inside a muscle car. He didn't have that Japanese name for nothing.

"So far," he said, writing notes onto a handy napkin, "we have three clues. First, we know that someone broke into the student council file and moved three thousand dollars out of it. Second, we think someone got into our class marks and raised Spike Gruber to a 92."

"Are you sure about that?" I asked.

"Just guessing, right now. Still, we both know there's no way Spike could get that grade honestly, right?"

"Right," I agreed. "What about clue number three?"

"Someone has been trashing the library's files, at least that's what your old girlfriend says."

"So what?"

"So, maybe nothing. I'm just trying to lay out everything we know. Maybe it will be easier to find a connection this way," Hacker said with a frown.

"Alright, so let's list out the suspects then," I said. "We know that Mrs. Layton didn't do it."

"No, all we really know is that she wasn't doing it tonight. But it doesn't make much sense for her to steal the money. It was just too easy for us to trace it to her. Maybe she was just practising for a bigger haul later on."

"You really think so?" I asked.

"Well, no," he said, shaking his head. "I don't think she's smart enough to pull off a major computer crime."

"But she's the computer teacher," I pointed out.

"She's *only* a teacher, Cole," Hacker said. He was looking at me like I was about as smart as a dung beetle. "Her password was about as simple as your toenail."

"So who else, then?"

"Well, there's you and me of course," he said, like I didn't know that already, "Spike Gruber . . ."

"He hasn't got two brain cells to rub together," I said.

"Maybe not, but he might have a friend that could help him. Besides, Spike would love to throw the blame on you. He's not exactly your best buddy," Hacker said.

"Not since I pulled him off your face back in Grade six," I said.

"Yeah, but you didn't have to beat him up after that," he laughed.

"Hey, I just try to look out for my friends," I said. I admit, I had to smile when I remembered it.

"Maybe if I can solve this thing, we can call it even," Hacker replied. "But there must be someone we're not thinking of. So far, this doesn't add up to anything at all."

"How about the school janitor?" I offered. "Lindsay said that he's taking courses in computers."

"Well, he does have a master key for the school. That means that he could get access to the labs whenever he wanted, but I still doubt it." Hacker thought for a moment. "We need to think of someone else with a key to the labs. There's either the library or the main lab on the second floor."

It was like a firecracker exploded in my head. "I've got it!" I shouted.

"Got what?" Hacker asked.

"I've got the person with the key! I'm sure of it!"

"Well, who is it?" Hacker asked.

"Just follow me," I said, tossing the empty coffee cup into the trash. "Sometimes when a genius like you gets stumped, a normal guy like me can still come up with an answer. It's like I keep telling you — I'm not as dumb as I look."

CHAPTER 8

Three Hackers

I came storming out of Tim Hortons with Hacker right on my heels. We ran across the street and through the doors of the school. I was headed straight for the library. Hacker moved faster than I thought his short legs could carry him.

"What do you want in the library?" Hacker asked when I told him where we were headed.

"Lindsay."

"I thought Lindsay shot you down last year."

"This isn't the time for jokes, Hacker," I told him. "I want to see Lindsay because she has a key to the library."

Hacker looked at me with a big grin. My flash of brain power was the first real break we'd had since all of this started.

In a few seconds we were just outside the doors of the library. One look inside and we stopped cold.

"Who's that on the computer?" Hacker whispered to me.

"I can't tell," I whispered back. "Try to stay out of sight until we can see who they are. Don't let Lindsay see you, no matter what." It was so quiet in the halls that I was afraid our breathing would give us away.

In the library, there were three guys back on the far wall by the computers. Lindsay was with them. They seemed to be gathered around one of the machines. We still couldn't make out who they were. The lights in the library were off since it was supposed to be closed. I could tell from the size of the guys that they were no Grade 9 pipsqueaks.

Hacker and I stayed as low as possible while still

being able to see the people through the windows in the library doors. We kept our eyes glued to them, hoping to make out some details. I had a feeling that these three were the answer to our problem.

Finally, one of the guys turned around to say something to Lindsay. I couldn't hear the words, but I knew the face right away.

"It's Maniac," I whispered.

"Cole, sometimes your luck is better than my brains," Hacker told me. "I bet at least one of the other guys is Spike Gruber. But who could the third one be?"

No sooner had Hacker whispered the question than we had an answer. The other two turned around and we could just barely make them out. The light was very dim, just streetlights shining through the rear windows. Still, it was enough. One of the other guys was Spike, all right, and the kid at the keyboard was Erik Jones.

"Who's that guy?" asked Hacker.

"My neighbour," I said. "Maniac's little brother."

Hacker had to chuckle to himself. "And your dad wants you to be like him?"

"It's no joke, Hacker. Erik was got into university early because he's so smart."

"I have a hunch he's not doing his homework on *that* computer."

"So you think we caught three hackers, eh?" I said.

"Cole, I'm going to go to the other computer lab and tap into the network. We need to see what they're up to. This could be the break we need," he said, sounding excited. "You wait here while I go downstairs," he added. "Don't let those guys turn off the machine until I get back."

With that, Hacker quietly tiptoed until he was out of earshot. He was gone before I even had a chance to think: how was I supposed to stop them from turning off the machine? There were three of them and only one of me. Even worse, Maniac is the biggest tackle our team has ever had. Me, I'm the smallest quarterback in the zone.

I watched them for what seemed like forever. It was probably only about ten minutes at the most. All that time I kept wondering how long Hacker was going to take. The library itself was quiet. Then

Lindsay checked her watch and said something to the others. She started making gestures that looked like she wanted them all out of there.

Spike said something back. He had a scowl on his face. It was as if he needed a little more time for something. I was afraid that he might turn the computer off right then. If he did, we'd never find out what he was doing on it.

Hacker wasn't around, so it was up to me. In a split second I crashed through the library door. The sound was enough to make them all jump.

The only problem was — what now?

CHAPTER 9

A Threat or a Promise?

We all stared at one another. Somebody had to make the first move, but didn't know what move to make.

So Lindsay was the first to speak. "The library is closed, Cole," she said.

"Interesting that it's only closed to me, don't you think?" I shot back. "My guess is that you and your stupid boyfriend are up to something."

"Hey, watch your mouth," spat Spike. "Don't

talk to my girlfriend like that." He got up and started moving towards me.

At least with all of them looking at me they couldn't turn off the machine. I just needed to stall them until Hacker came back.

"Sorry about that," I said, smiling. I needed to waste as much time as possible. Besides, I didn't like the odds of one-against-four.

"Funny seeing you here, Erik," I said.

Maniac's brother smiled at me. "I just came in to help Spike with a computer assignment," he said.

"Oh, I bet," I told him. "That must be how Spike got his 92 from Mrs. Layton."

"I got mine the same way you got your 38, Cole," Spike broke in.

Now I've got him, I thought to myself.

"How did you know I only got a 38? I never told you my mark. I only told you that it was bad. The only person I told was Hacker, and he'd never tell you."

"Lucky guess," said Spike, smiling and trying to cover up his mistake.

"You know what I think, Spike?" I said moving

73

between the four of them and the computers. "I think you broke Layton's password. I think you were screwing around with the marks. I think you moved the money out of the student council accounts and set me up to take the fall."

I glanced at the computer screen once I got close enough. There was a list of student council files on the screen. My guesses were right.

"Spike, he knows . . ." Erik began, shooting a look at his partner in crime.

"He doesn't know nothing. All he's got is a

bunch of wild guesses," Spike shot back nervously. "He just wants somebody else to go down for taking the three grand."

I smirked. "How did you know it was three grand?" I asked him.

Erik looked like a deer in headlights, eyes as big as dinner plates. Maniac looked confused. Spike was definitely looking angry. He was getting caught by his own words and he knew it.

"A little birdie told me, Cole," said Spike stepping a little closer to me. "You can't pin this on us anyway. Who would ever believe that two dumb football players pulled off a computer crime?"

This was getting too tense for comfort. Where the heck was Hacker when I needed him? Spike was confessing the whole thing, but the only one to hear it was me.

"So you admit it then?" I asked.

"We don't admit nothing," grunted Maniac. "You ain't got proof."

"That's right," said Erik. He looked a little more confident now. "You can't prove a thing. You can't even prove that you saw me here in the library."

The three of them began to laugh and that made me mad. The problem is — when I get mad I start to do really stupid things.

"I've got the proof right here," I said, pointing to the computer near me.

"Erik, you left the file list on the screen!" snapped Spike.

"Relax," said Erik. "We just have to turn off the machine and all his proof goes . . . poof."

"Over my dead body," I said, determined not to let that happen.

"Is that a threat or a promise?" asked Spike. The three of them had me badly outnumbered. Lindsay wasn't doing anything to stop this. She just stared at her feet.

"I'm ready for you," I said. I tried to pretend I could take on all of them.

"If you've got that much of a death wish, consider it granted," said Spike. "Maniac, why don't you show Cole exactly why you earned that name." Spike turned back to me as Maniac cracked his knuckles. "This is just a fraction of the pain you'll feel once the team finds out that the money is gone."

Maniac came for me. He was way bigger than me, but I had speed on my side. He tried to slam into me from the front, but I dodged sideways. I avoided the first attack, but I needed to make the next move. While Maniac was off balance, I rushed him. I threw a wild flying tackle and caught him in the side. We went crashing into a low shelf and books went flying everywhere.

For whatever reason I guess I thought Maniac would stay down after that. He didn't. Faster than I thought possible he rolled over and tried to get to his feet. He didn't even look winded from my attack. If he got up before I did, then this was all

over. Not bothering to get all the way up, I jumped on his back from a crouched position. I managed to knock him back onto the floor, but he was far from out.

Where was Hacker? Maniac was almost twice my size. Even if I could manage to keep him down, Spike and Erik were bound to jump in. With me out of the way they could easily shut down the computer.

Even with me covering his back, Maniac got up on one knee. I tried to push my body down on him, but he could probably bench-press heavier weights than me. He hooked one of his enormous arms through mine and flipped me off him. I landed right on my face. The fall totally knocked the wind out of me. Even worse, I felt him jump on my back and put me in a hold.

I swear, this guy weighed as much as a small Toyota. I pushed and shoved with my arms, trying to get up. I swung my legs as much as I could trying to connect with something. I just couldn't get free. It got a million times worse as I felt his forearm wrap around my neck.

The others laughed now. "Don't hurt him too

much, Maniac. Leave some for the rest of the team," jeered Spike.

I was afraid of that fate even more. I doubled my efforts to get him off of me. I was flopping around like a fish pulled from the water, gasping for air. It didn't bother Maniac in the slightest. I tried to grab for his hair. Normally you just don't do that, but this was far from a fair fight. All I wanted to do was breathe for a little while longer.

Before I could reach far enough, Maniac started to flex his arm muscles. He was crushing my neck and I couldn't breathe. I started pounding my fists into his arm, but it was no use. I wasn't having any effect on him. There was only one thing left to do.

I bit him — hard!

"You dirty little mother …" he shouted. He let go of my neck as he felt his arm for the damage. I scrambled away and tried to get my breath back. I could taste blood.

I was just getting to my feet when Spike stepped up. He sucker-punched me right in the eye. The punch sent me sprawling on the floor. I was losing the willpower to keep fighting back. That was when

Maniac got back on top of me. This time he wasn't toying with me. This time he was just going to smash my head into the floor until brains leaked out of my ears.

Grabbing me by the shirt, he pulled me up and said, "I'm really going to enjoy this, punk."

He slammed me into the floor. Searing pain shot through my head. There was nothing I could do to protect myself. I knew it deep inside. This was the end of Cole Walsh.

He lifted me up and slammed my head down again. I was seeing stars now. One more of those and I was going to black out. I waited for the next slam, but it never came. I didn't know how, but Maniac went flying off me.

CHAPTER 10

Layton to the Rescue

My ears were ringing, but I tried to recover as best I could. Holding one hand to my head I struggled to my feet. When my vision cleared, I saw Maniac twisting on the floor in pain.

Hacker was on top of him. Maniac's arm was wrenched up behind his back. Hacker was twisting it with everything he had. I thought he might break Maniac's arm right off. Maniac just kept screaming for Hacker to stop.

"All right, let him go," said a stern voice from the door. It was Mrs. Layton.

Hacker released Maniac, but not before giving his arm one last twist.

"He broke my arm!" blubbered Maniac.

"No, I didn't, you moron," said Hacker, picking up his glasses from the floor. Then Hacker turned to me and said, "Why didn't you wait for me?"

"Erik was about to turn off the computer," I replied. "I was just trying to stall them until you got back."

"You could have saved yourself the big fight," Hacker told me. "We have a log downstairs of everything they did tonight."

I touched the swelling around my eye. I rubbed the back of my head and felt some blood from where it was smashed into the floor. I had to wonder why Hacker's words of wisdom were always too late to help. "So I wrestled with these guys for nothing?"

"Next time," said Hacker, "if you need a workout, go lift some weights."

Mrs. Layton broke into our talk and turned to the others. "All right, Manny," said Mrs. Layton. It was always strange to hear someone use Maniac's real name. "Stop whining about your arm and tell me how you got into this. I want a straight story from all of you."

"I told him not to do it," Maniac sniffled. "I didn't know about the money until after . . ."

"Who's they?" Hacker asked.

Maniac glanced at Spike for a second and stopped talking.

"All right, Spike, I guess it's your turn to talk," said Mrs. Layton. "It was the three of you wasn't it?"

Spike nodded.

"Who set up the program that broke my password?" she asked, looking at the three of them. Then Mrs. Layton answered her own question. "Erik, it was you, wasn't it."

Erik twisted his body and looked at the ground. There was silence while we all waited.

At last Erik began to talk. "It all started as a joke. We were going to give the money back after we had a little fun with Cole. The money is still in the bank. We moved it to a new account, that's all."

"I'm surprised a student like you would get into something like this," Mrs. Layton said.

"It was just a joke," offered Spike. "We were in here one night to pick up Lindsay. We were just kind of goofing around when I told Erik that you kept all our marks and stuff on the school's computers. He said he could bust in and change the grades around. We dared him to try it, and that's how it started."

"But not how it finished," said Mrs. Layton in a stern voice. "How did you get into the library?"

The three of them looked sheepishly at Lindsay,

who was busy trying not to get noticed. It was Spike who actually laid the blame. "She's got the key."

Mrs. Layton stared a hole right through her. "You might as well tell me your part in this mess, Lindsay."

"I thought it was stupid right from the start," Lindsay said. "I only gave them the key because the three of them kept bugging me. I mean, Spike threatened me, but I didn't have anything else to do with it."

"But you knew about the three grand," I said.

Lindsay couldn't even meet my eyes. "That was only a joke, Cole. They were going to put it back right after you got in trouble over the missing money."

"Real funny joke," I said. Why would they even risk giving back the money just to make a joke? It didn't make sense to me. "Whose idea was it to blame this on me?" I asked.

"We had to blame it on someone," Erik said. "When Spike saw that we could pin this on you, well, so much the better. Spike wanted to get even with you and your buddy here. He says you beat him up, like, six years ago. Believe me, we were going to give the money back."

"And my name is Santa Claus," I told him.

"That's enough, Cole," said Mrs. Layton. "I think we've gone about as far as we can right now. I want to see all of you in the office on Monday morning, including you Erik. All of you had better bring your parents. I'm not sure whether the principal will call the police. But I can tell you that you won't get off easy."

"What about us?" asked Hacker.

Mrs. Layton turned and scanned him with those mean eyes of hers. "I'm still not happy that you broke my password, young man. But I think I've got a deal for you. You help me protect the school's computer system and I'll let you off. Try and make the program one that nobody, not even you, can break into."

She turned and looked me over, too.

"As for you, Cole, you had better get yourself cleaned up. If you were the one who solved this mess, I suspect the principal might want to shake your hand come Monday morning."

CHAPTER 11

No One Is Perfect

The principal really did shake my hand on Monday morning. Ms. Hawthorne said she had always trusted me. I wasn't sure if I could believe that one. She also said she was glad to see my name cleared. That one I did believe.

I wasn't in the office when she dealt with Spike and the others. From what I heard, there weren't any handshakes.

Even though they did give back all the money,

Ms. Hawthorne slammed them pretty hard. Spike and Maniac were kicked out for two weeks. They were also cut from any team sports for the rest of the year.

Erik got off with a warning and a letter to his college. It seemed strange that the brains behind the whole thing should get off the easiest. I guess that's just how it works.

Lindsay was fired from her job at the library. She blamed Spike for that, but I think she should have blamed herself. I mean, she had a chance to go out with me — and she had no problem saying no to that.

The next week, Hacker helped Mrs. Layton program some super security system for the school's network. He says that he lived up to his promise. Even *he* can't break into it now.

The new football equipment came in last week. There were uniforms, tackling sleds, the works. The team treated me like a hero once they heard what happened in those few days. They weren't quite so kind to Spike Gruber when they found out his role in the scam.

Even my father has gotten off my back in the past little while. When the news came out about Erik Jones, he must have felt lucky to have me for a son. Maybe he's starting to see that there's more to a person than just brains.

I'm starting to see that myself. When Hacker starts acting like he's so much smarter than me, I just don't let him. After all, who was it that solved the crime?

Things are more equal between us now. Hacker doesn't feel like he owes me anything anymore. Ever since Grade six he had been trying to find a way to pay me back for pulling Spike off his face. Now that he pulled Maniac off me, we're even. In fact, I found out that I'm not that far behind him in our computer marks.

"I've got good news for you," Hacker told me just two days ago. We were playing a computer game at his house.

"Yeah?"

"I went back through the marks in computer class and found out what happened."

"It was that lousy project mark. We already know that," I said.

"No, it was Spike who bombed the project. They switched some of the marks around and gave you his," explained Hacker.

"And . . ."

"And," he said pausing for effect. "Your real midterm mark in computer class was a 79."

"Really?" I said, surprised.

"Would I kid you about something like that?" asked Hacker.

"So what about your mark?" I replied.

"Mrs. Layton says she'll give me some bonus marks for setting up that new security. That means I'll have a 99 on the report card."

"Oh? Why not a full one hundred percent?"

"Because no one is perfect, Cole," Hacker said with a smile. "Not even a computer."

ABOUT THE AUTHOR

ALEX KROPP is the author of a number of short stories and non-fiction works used by publishers such as Scholastic in their educational programs. As well, he designed several of the workbooks and wrote activity-book materials for CBC's *Mr. Dressup* project.

Alex became interested in computers early in life, playing games on an ancient Atari 800 and then programming in Windows using Basic and C languages. He took his diploma as a systems analyst from Seneca College and now works for IBM in Toronto. *Hacker* is his first full-length novel. In this book, he was able to combine his knowledge of computer systems with his love of writing.